Southampton

Bremerhaven
Bad Harzburg
Sankt Andreasberg

First published in the United States in 2021
by Eerdmans Books for Young Readers,
an imprint of Wm. B. Eerdmans Publishing Co.
Grand Rapids, Michigan

www.eerdmans.com/youngreaders

Text © Dieter Böge
Illustrations © Elsa Klever
Originally published in Germany as *189*
© 2020 Aladin Verlag, an imprint of Thienemann-Esslinger, Stuttgart

English-language translation copyright © Laura Watkinson 2021

Manufactured in China

29 28 27 26 25 24 23 22 21   1 2 3 4 5 6 7 8 9

Library of Congress Cataloging-in-Publication Data

Names: Böge, Dieter, 1958- author. | Klever, Elsa, 1985- illustrator. |
   Watkinson, Laura, translator.
Title: 189 canaries / Dieter Böge ; [illustrated by] Elsa Klever ;
   translated by Laura Watkinson.
Other titles: 189. English | One hundred and eighty-nine canaries
Description: Grand Rapids, Michigan : Eerdmans Books for Young Readers,
   2021. | Originally published in Germany by Aladin Verlag in 2020 under
   title: 189. | Audience: Ages 6 -10. | Summary: In the nineteenth
   century, a caged canary that sings in the silver mines travels with
   a canary dealer from the Harz Mountains of Germany to a new home in
   Poughkeepsie, New York. Includes notes on the history of canaries.
Identifiers: LCCN 2021003751 | ISBN 9780802855749 (hardcover)
Subjects: LCSH: Carnaries—Juvenile fiction. | CYAC: Canaries—Fiction. |
   Voyages and travels—Fiction.
Classification: LCC PZ10.3.B63715 Aah 2021 | DDC [E]—dc23
LC record available at https://lccn.loc.gov/2021003751

Illustrations created with mixed media

er Böge • Elsa Klever

189
CANARIES

TRANSLATED BY
Laura Watkinson

EERDMANS BOOKS FOR YOUNG READERS

GRAND RAPIDS, MICHIGAN

This is the story of a long journey,
but I'll keep it as short as I can,
because it has such a lovely ending.

In a cozy room that smells a little like freshly sawed wood, a canary sits in his cage and looks out the window. He can see the sky and almost half of a large spruce tree, and—in the distance—a forest on a hill. The cage and the room are his home. Right now, he's alone, because the people he lives with are busy doing other things. He can hear the voices of the women and the children in the house and in the garden. In the evening, he'll be able to hear the men again, too.

During the day, the men dig deep underground inside a mine, looking for silver. The canary has often gone with them under the earth and sung for them. When the air starts to run out, he stops singing. Then the miners know they need to bring themselves and the canary to safety. They leave the underground tunnels and take their birds out with them into the fresh air. Today, though, our canary has the day off.

After dinner, the people will come to his room. They'll open the cage door and talk to him, and he'll start singing. They'll sit down and cut pieces of wood to the right size and put together small cages for the canaries they breed after their long day at work. The canary will fly around the room, perching in the new cages and performing all the fancy sequences of notes that canaries learn in the Harz Mountains. His people will listen to him sing.

That evening, a stranger comes to join them. He talks to the people, shakes their hands, and gives them a few coins. When he leaves the room, he reaches for the bird's wooden cage, closes the little door, puts a thin cloth over the cage, and carries it out of the house with our canary inside.

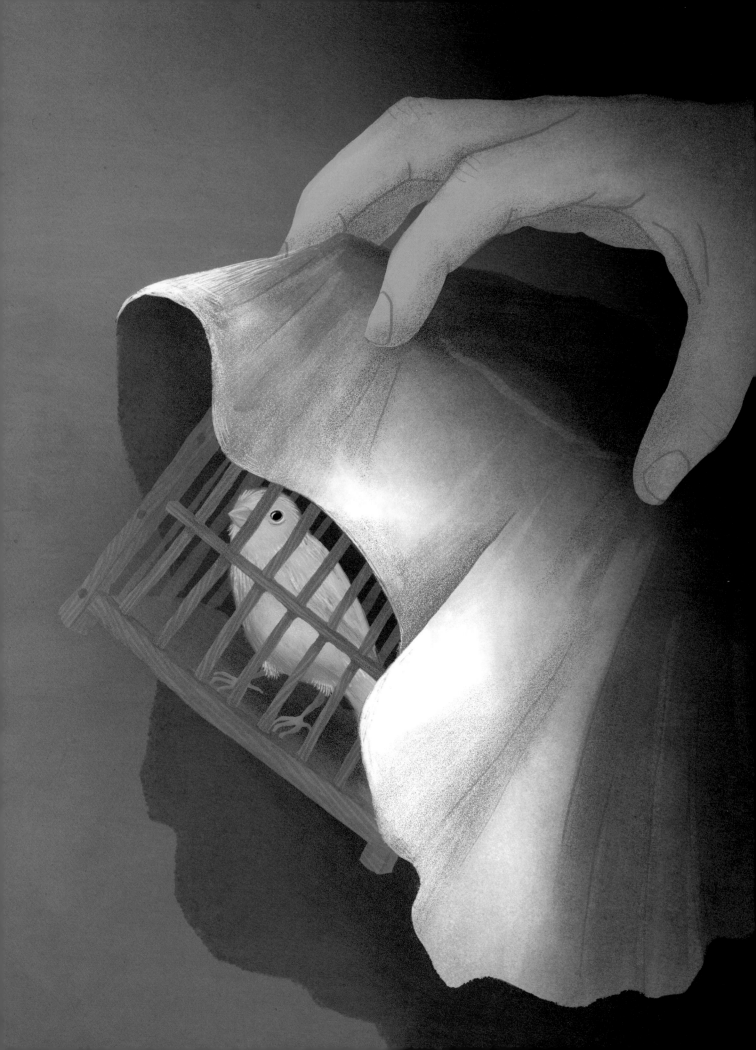

The man is a bird dealer. When he gets back to his inn, he attaches the cage to a rack that already has one hundred eighty-eight other transport cages hanging from it. Inside those cages are one hundred eighty-eight other canaries, which he has bought from other local breeders.

The next morning he feeds the birds and gives them water, and then he carries the rack with one hundred eighty-nine birds on his back through the forest and over the same hill that our canary could see through the window in his room at home.

On their way through the forest, the birds can't see the stony ground, the trees, or the sky. The dealer has tied a sturdy sheet of cloth around the rack, so that they're protected from the wind and aren't afraid of the strange surroundings. Each of the birds sits inside its own little cage.

The light looks gray under the canvas cover. They can hear the gravel under the dealer's boots. With every step, the rack sways left, then right. The cages rub against each other, and the thin wooden bars creak quietly, but they're strong enough not to break.

The canary hears a woodpecker hammering away in the forest and, in the distance, the call of a cuckoo. Then the clattering of hooves, horses snorting, chains rattling nearby, human voices coming and going. The dealer stops walking, and the little songbirds under the canvas keep very quiet.

The journey continues with a horse and cart. The dealer sits up front with the driver. With one hand, he holds on tightly to the backpack on the cart. A pig grunts sleepily next to the baggage, wrinkles its nose, and sniffs the cloth, but it doesn't open its eyes, because the sun is high in the sky by now and it's dazzling. It's getting warm under the canvas.

When the dealer finally lifts the sheet to check on the birds, the canary sees strangers all around, and houses and shadows. A locomotive is steaming and hissing on the platform. The dealer quickly ties up the cloth again, lifts the backpack into the railroad car, and climbs up after it. A whistle shrieks, the doors close with a bang, and the train starts moving. *Ta-tamm-tamm, ta-tamm-tamm, ta-tamm-tamm, ta-tamm-tamm.*

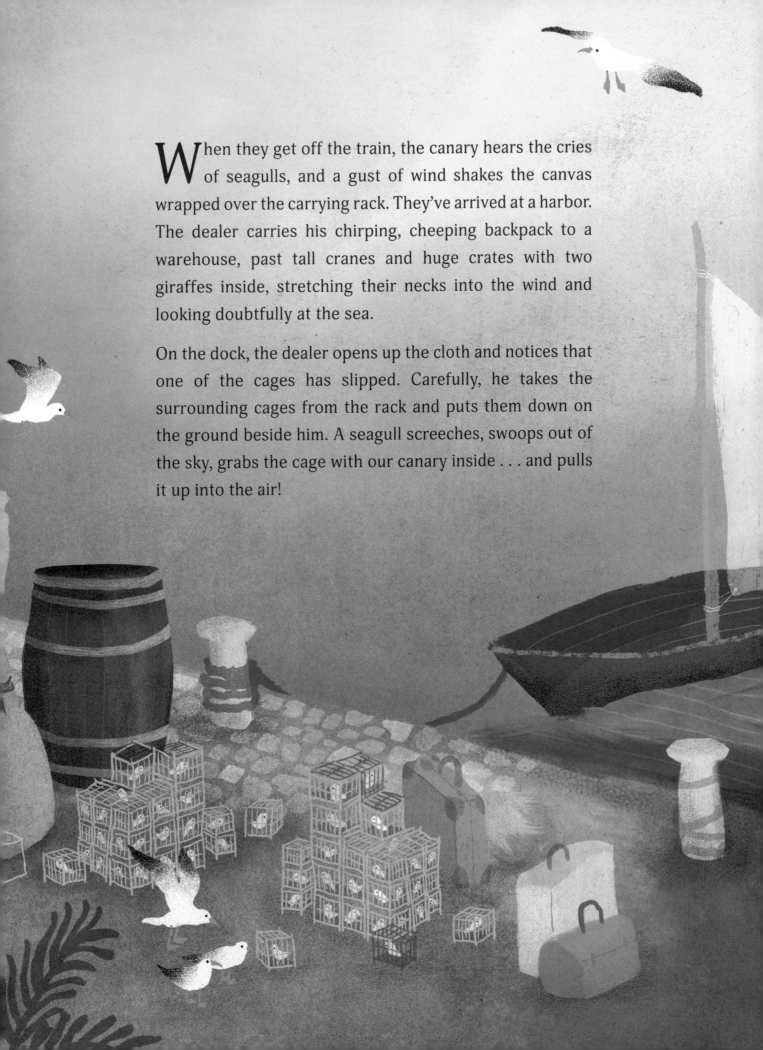

When they get off the train, the canary hears the cries of seagulls, and a gust of wind shakes the canvas wrapped over the carrying rack. They've arrived at a harbor. The dealer carries his chirping, cheeping backpack to a warehouse, past tall cranes and huge crates with two giraffes inside, stretching their necks into the wind and looking doubtfully at the sea.

On the dock, the dealer opens up the cloth and notices that one of the cages has slipped. Carefully, he takes the surrounding cages from the rack and puts them down on the ground beside him. A seagull screeches, swoops out of the sky, grabs the cage with our canary inside . . . and pulls it up into the air!

The dealer curses and throws a stone at the thief, missing his target, and the seagull flies away. But the load is too heavy. Above the harbor, the seagull loosens its grip and lets go. The little wooden cage lands in the water with a splash and floats on the waves, its door hanging at an angle.

The canary flies out and sits on top of the cage, shaking the saltwater from his feathers. In the sky, the seagulls circle and squabble. A sailor fishes the shipwrecked bird and the cage out of the water, perches him on his tattooed arm, shields him with his hand, and takes him back to the dealer.

That night, the canary dreams about his peaceful room in the forest and the voices in the house and the cry of a seagull flying past the window. The next morning, the dealer carries the birds, all safely wrapped up, across a wobbly gangplank and onto the deck of an ocean liner, and then he looks for a spot between decks. The air is stuffy, and there are only a few small windows. For eight days, he takes constant care of his birds and keeps the cages nice and clean, while the pounding engines propel the heavy steamship across the Atlantic.

When they reach New York Harbor, the dealer leaves the ship and takes his goods to a building where some strangers are waiting. They open the backpack and divide the birds among themselves. Our canary, along with seven others, is transported away inside a box. They rumble in a streetcar through the noise of the big city. A doorbell rings, the box is unpacked, and the eight canaries are placed in a beautiful cage in the display window of a pet store.

Before long, the doorbell rings again. A woman and a man enter the store, point at different birds, and finally decide on our canary. They take him home with them in the small transport cage.

A girl is waiting at the front door of the house to welcome the bird. She carries the cage down the hallway, up the stairs, and into a room that smells a little like freshly sawed wood. By the window, there's a big new birdcage. Its door is open wide. There's a canary sitting on top of the cage. It looks over at them. When it starts to sing, it's a song that it could only have learned in one place in the whole world.

"That's Joe," says the girl. "And what would you like us to call you?"

Our little canary is home.

AFTERWORD: NOTES ON THE HISTORY OF CANARIES

Canaries are named after the Canary Islands, which lie off the coast of Africa in the Atlantic Ocean. Yellow-green wild canaries fly around free on the islands, twittering away for their own pleasure. They have very good hearing, and the male birds learn new songs every year. The female wild canaries have enjoyed the variety of the males' beautiful singing for thousands of years—and people love to listen to them as well.

In the late Middle Ages, Spanish sailors brought some of these canaries to mainland Europe.

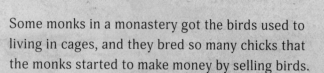

Some monks in a monastery got the birds used to living in cages, and they bred so many chicks that the monks started to make money by selling birds.

The best singers soon became very popular in the castles of kings and princes, where they sang for them and their guests. The cages that the birds lived in often looked like little palaces, with all kinds of glittering turrets, swings, and mirrors.

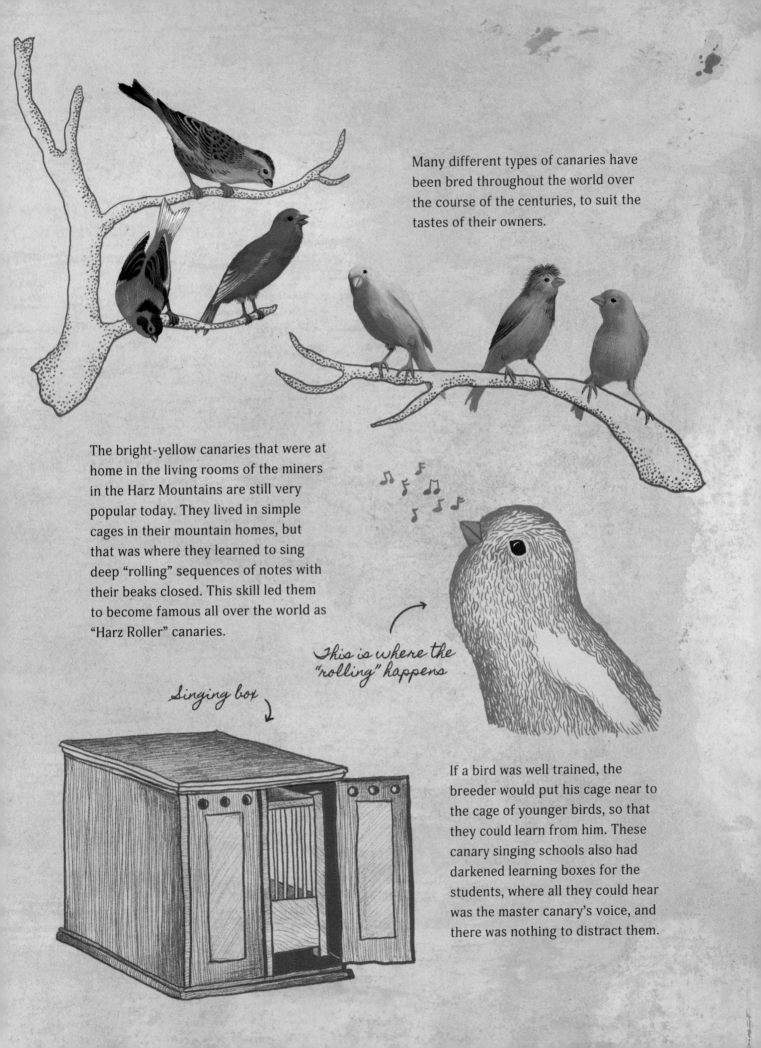

Many different types of canaries have been bred throughout the world over the course of the centuries, to suit the tastes of their owners.

The bright-yellow canaries that were at home in the living rooms of the miners in the Harz Mountains are still very popular today. They lived in simple cages in their mountain homes, but that was where they learned to sing deep "rolling" sequences of notes with their beaks closed. This skill led them to become famous all over the world as "Harz Roller" canaries.

This is where the "rolling" happens

Singing box

If a bird was well trained, the breeder would put his cage near to the cage of younger birds, so that they could learn from him. These canary singing schools also had darkened learning boxes for the students, where all they could hear was the master canary's voice, and there was nothing to distract them.

In the nineteenth century, customers all over the world were eager to buy canaries from the Harz Mountains, and they were willing to pay as much as a Harz miner could earn in a week underground. First, though, the dealer had to hike through the mountains with his heavy backpack full of birds, taking good care of his singing companions throughout the entire journey, which could take weeks. In the year 1882 alone, 120,000 canaries were shipped across the Atlantic Ocean to New York in this way.

Water for the sea journey

Food

Can for filling up the clay drinking bowl

Each canary's cage had its own clay drinking bowl, and the thin base boards could be slid out to the side in order to clean the cage. Seven of these cages were attached next to one another, all in a row.

Nine of these rows were stacked on top of one another. Seven times nine is sixty-three, and three of these stacks could fit onto a rack. That made one hundred eighty-nine cages in total, stacked up and held together with a cloth, which the dealer carried on his back for days. And inside each of those cages was a precious Harz Roller.

Rack

Vorsicht!
Lebende Vögel!

Clay drinking bowl

Food bowl

The miners from the Harz also took the canaries into the mines as protection while they were working. If there wasn't enough fresh air coming into the underground tunnels, the little birds noticed the lack of oxygen much sooner than the miners—and they stopped singing. That was a warning for the workers, so that they could get themselves to safety in time. Of course they took their tiny lifesavers with them as they escaped—and they were very relieved when the birds started to sing again.

Miner's lamp (also known as a frog lamp)

In Sankt Andreasberg in the Harz Mountains, there's a museum with live canaries and a very good exhibition about the history of the Harz Roller. We would like to thank Mr. Jochen Klähn, the director of the Harz Roller Museum, for his expert advice and kind support.

— Dieter Böge and Elsa Klever

DIETER BÖGE is a children's book author, painter, and translator. His books have been nominated for the German Youth Literature Award and selected for the International Youth Library's White Ravens catalog. *189 Canaries* began when Dieter discovered a photo of 189 canvas-covered birdcages on a wooden rack, which made him curious about their story. Dieter lives in Germany. *189 Canaries* is his English-language debut.

ELSA KLEVER is an illustrator and fine artist whose books include *Taxi Ride with Victor* (Prestel Junior). She was the winner of the 2015 Austrian Children's Book Award and has been shortlisted twice for the World Illustration Award. Elsa lives in Germany. Visit her website at elsaklever.de or follow her on Instagram @elsaklever.

LAURA WATKINSON translates books into English from German, Italian, and Dutch. Her translations have received numerous honors, including three Mildred L. Batchelder Awards and the Vondel Translation Prize. She is the founder of the Dutch chapter of the Society of Children's Book Writers and Illustrators (SBCWI). Laura lives in Amsterdam. Visit her website at laurawatkinson.com or follow her on twitter @Laura_Wat.

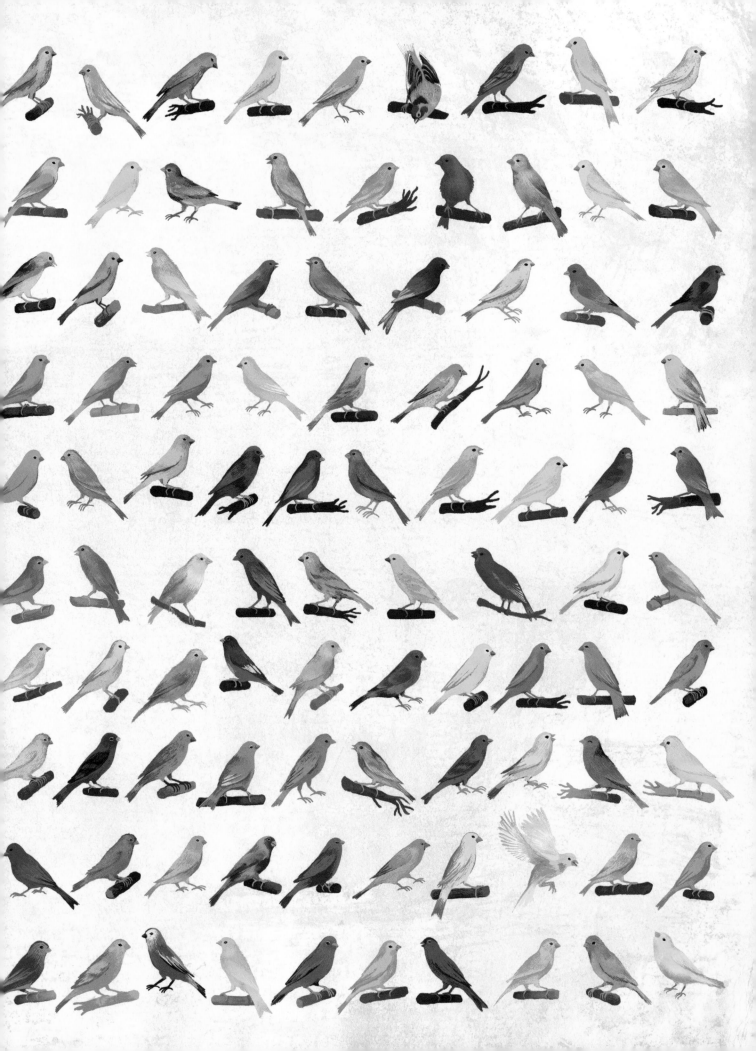

Poughkeepsie

New York